Peter Penguin and Friends

Short Stories, Fuzzy Animals and Life Lessons

Norma MacDonald

Karma for Kids Books

Peter Penguin and Friends
Short Stories, Fuzzy Animals, and Life Lessons

Copyright © 2016 Norma MacDonald

First Edition

Published by: Find Your Way Publishing, Inc.
PO BOX 667
Norway, ME 04268 U.S.A.
www.findyourwaypublishing.com

ISBN-13: 978-0-9849322-7-6

ISBN-10: 0-9849322-7-5

Library of Congress Control Number: 2016937300

DEDICATION

This book is dedicated to all of the people trying to make the world a better place. You are making a positive difference!

"Sow a thought, and you reap and act; Sow an act, and you reap a habit; Sow a habit, and you reap a character; Sow a character, and you reap destiny."
~ Samuel Smiles

TABLE OF CONTENTS

ABOUT THIS BOOK

Welcome to our Karma for Kids Books Series. We are very grateful that you picked up this book. We believe together we can make a positive difference, one child at a time. We strive to instill important life lessons in the lives of young children. We are firm believers in Karma and think that if this simple Law of the Universe is taught to children at a young age, their lives will have the potential to be absolutely amazing.

We once knew a dog named Karma. She was a beautiful, yellow Labrador retriever. It wasn't until after she passed, at 11 years old (God bless her loyal soul.), that we realized just how fitting her name really was.

Karma is indeed a retriever.

Whatever we threw out, Karma was always happy to bring it back to us. It didn't matter what it was, she always brought it back. If we threw out garbage, she'd bring it back without question. If we threw out the most beautiful dog toy, she'd bring it back. It's the same in life. Whatever you send out, is what you will get back. Guaranteed. Every time. Our Karma for Kids Book Series hopes to instill this easy-to-understand Law of the Universe into the lives of children at a young age. The Universe wants to happily bring you all that your heart desires, and it will, effortlessly. But first, you've got to throw out what you want it to bring back to you so that it can! Have fun with this and watch the magic happen. God bless!

Find all of Norma MacDonald's Karma for Kids Books at Amazon.com.

For more of our Karma for Kids books please visit us at:

www.karmaforkidsbooks.wordpress.com

or

www.findyourwaypublishing.com

Other books that we recommend to help children learn important life lessons:

Billy Brown Bear and Friends: Short Stories, Fuzzy Animals, and Life Lessons by Norma MacDonald

Humble Heron and Friends: Short Stories, Fuzzy Animals, and Life Lessons by Norma MacDonald

Guaranteed Success for Kindergarten; 50 Easy Things You Can Do Today! by Marrae Kimball

Guaranteed Success for Grade School; 50 Easy Things You Can Do Today! by Marrae Kimball

The Secret Combination to Middle School: Real Advice from Real Kids, Ideas for Success, and Much More! by Marrae Kimball

Thank you!

Peter Penguin and Friends

Short Stories, Fuzzy Animals and Life Lessons

Norma MacDonald

Karma for Kids Books

NORMA MACDONALD

CHAPTER ONE

The Money Tree

PETER PENGUIN SOMETIMES felt jealous that his friends seemed to have cooler toys and games than him. Edgar Elephant just got a new skateboard, Francine Flamingo always had the newest sneakers, and Henry Hamster had a trampoline! Peter Penguin had an old skateboard, he had the same pair of shoes from the year before, and his backyard wasn't even big enough to fit a trampoline, but he did have a swing set.

Whenever the group of friends was making plans to all hang out together, Peter Penguin never suggested his house. He was too embarrassed to invite his friends over. He worried that there would be nothing fun to do.

"Hey mom," said Peter one day, "I've had these old sneakers for a quite a while now, and I saw these really cool new ones that are yellow and navy blue checkered and I think I could use a new pair."

"Do your shoes still fit?" She asked.

"Yes."

"Are there any holes in them?"

"No."

"Are they comfortable?"

"Yes."

"Then why do you need a new pair? Money doesn't grow on trees, Peter."

Peter felt defeated and went to school wearing his old sneakers. It's not that he didn't like his old shoes, they were his favorite pair he ever had, but sometimes he just wished that his mom would buy him a new pair so he had more options.

He decided to try again, the next day, with his mom.

"Hey mom," he said, "I saw, today, that the sneakers are now on sale and I would never wear them outside when it is rainy or muddy, so they will last me a long time."

"Peter Penguin, we talked about this yesterday. Money does not grow on trees. If you want those sneakers, you can buy them yourself."

"But I have no money, how will I buy them?"

Peter Penguin knew his mother always said that money doesn't grow on trees, but now he wished that it did. Then he would be able to go out and grab a couple dollars from a branch.

That night he dreamed that there was a giant money tree growing in his backyard. There were even one-hundred dollar bills on it! He couldn't reach the very top of the tree and that's where the largest amounts of money were. In his dream, Peter Penguin was raking piles of money into a great big pile. Once he filled up five garbage bags with money, he had enough to buy the new sneakers.

"I have an idea!" He announced when he woke up from the dream. Outside the leaves were changing color and falling off the trees. Everyone's lawns were covered by so many leaves that you could barely even see the grass!

Peter Penguin grabbed his coat and gloves and searched his garage for a rake. He knew there must be a rake in there somewhere. Finally, he saw it. It was all the way in the back of the garage under a bicycle he had outgrown years ago. "Hmmm," he said, "I don't really need this bike anymore."

He pulled the bike outside and tacked a sign onto it that said: "FOR SALE $20." And put it next to the curb. Peter Penguin went back into the garage to grab the rake and he waddled over to his next door neighbor's house.

"Good morning Mr. Owl," said Peter, "I noticed that your lawn is covered in fall leaves. Would you like me to rake it for you?"

Mr. Owl hooted. "Well, that is mighty nice of you Peter Penguin! An old owl like myself doesn't have the energy a young penguin like yourself does. I will give you five dollars to rake my yard!" He handed Peter a crisp five-dollar bill and Peter raked every leaf off of that lawn, that you wouldn't have even known it was autumn!

"Peter Penguin!" Called Miss Lizard across the street. "Can you rake my lawn next? I will also give you five dollars!"

After finishing bagging the last leaves on Mr. Owl's lawn, Peter ran across the street to Miss Lizard's yard. Now he had ten dollars!

"Hey Peter Penguin, is that your bike for sale?" Betty Buffalo who lives on the next block was walking by with her dad.

"Yes, it is."

"Dad can I please have it? You know I've been looking for a bike to ride. And this is a perfect size. I love it!"

Mr. Buffalo reached into his pocket and handed Peter Penguin twenty dollars. Now he had thirty dollars! All he needed was twenty more and then he could buy those sneakers! How many lawns was that? Well, if each lawn paid five dollars and five plus five is ten, then he needed to rake more four lawns. Although his hands hurt a little from all the raking, he knew he could do it. He was on a mission.

"Peter Penguin, what are you doing in Miss Lizard's front yard?"

Peter heard his mother calling from the front door. He ran home to explain his plan.

"You told me that if I wanted new sneakers, I had to pay for them myself, so I decided I would make money by helping the neighbors rake their yards and I also sold my old bike that was just sitting in the garage."

"That is very responsible of you, how much money have you made so far?"

"Thirty dollars!"

"And how much more do you need?"

"Just twenty, that means I only have to rake four more yards and I can buy new shoes!"

Mrs. Penguin was so proud of her son for learning that it takes hard work and responsibility to get the things you want, that she decided to pay him the twenty dollars once he raked his own front yard. "I'm so proud of you. I'll tell you what. If you help clean up our front yard, as nicely as you did the others, I will give you the twenty dollars you need to buy the sneakers."

Peter Penguin was so excited. When he finally had the right amount of money, more neighbors were asking him to rake the leaves from their yard. Once he finished raking the entire block, he had enough money to buy two pairs of shoes!

He ran to the shoe store and bought himself the pair of yellow and blue checkered sneakers and decided to save the rest of the money for the next time he wanted to buy something. Thanks to the money tree, he learned how to earn his own money since it really doesn't grow on trees.

CHAPTER TWO

THE CASE OF
THE LOST
IMAGINATION

HENRY HAMSTER LOVED PLAYING video games. His favorite type of video games were the racing ones. He liked to be in a car or boat or airplane zooming around a racetrack trying to be the fastest player. Whenever Henry had friends over to play, the first thing he did was turn on his

TV and video game system.

One day, after school, his best friend Edgar Elephant came over. Edgar's parents had to stay late at work, so he was going to Henry's house until they could pick him up.

"Check this game out!" Henry shouted enthusiastically. "It is my newest game. You get to design motorcycles and then race them on all different kinds of tracks. There is even a track that goes around the rings of Saturn! Let's play!"

Henry Hamster and Edgar Elephant picked up their video game controllers and chose their motorcycles. Henry picked a big one that was black with red, orange, and yellow flames going down each side. Edgar picked a smaller one that was blue with a neon yellow pinstripe on it.

The races went through the Grand Canyon,

around Saturn, and around the city of Paris.

"I'm bored of this game," said Edgar, "let's go outside and play catch."

"I don't really feel like going outside," said Henry, "want to play this football video game instead? It has some really cool graphics and it makes it look like it's real life!"

Before Edgar Elephant could answer, Henry Hamster hopped up and put the new game into the video game console. The menu appeared on the big TV screen and they both chose their teams.

Henry picked the Polar Vortex as his team. The team was made up of polar bears, penguins, and sea lions. The quarterback for the Vortex was a tall penguin and he was the best in the Animal Football League. They had all white uniforms with black numbers on them.

Edgar picked the Heat Wave as his team. On that team, there were scorpions, rattlesnakes, and camels. The quarterback was just a rookie, but the Heat Wave had the best defense in the league.

After playing all four quarters of the game, Edgar spoke up again. He said, "Can we go play outside now? It's so nice out and the sun is going to go down soon."

"Let's just do one more game!" Said Henry.

Edgar didn't feel like playing another video game, so he just watched as Henry put in a game where he had to race through a maze and collect stars. Before the game finished, Edgar's parents came and picked him up.

"See you tomorrow in school Henry!" Called Edgar as he was leaving, but Henry didn't even look away from the game he was playing on the TV screen.

The next day in school, Henry was telling all of his classmates about how much fun he and Edgar had playing video games.

"Racing around Saturn?!" Said Peter Penguin, "Sounds awesome!"

"A game between the Polar Vortex and the Heat Waves sounds even cooler!" Said Francine Flamingo.

"It was!" Said Henry, "Tell them how fun it was, Edgar!"

Everyone turned to look at Edgar. He shrugged and said, "Yeah, it was pretty cool, but we didn't really get to play outside before it got dark."

When it came time for recess everyone raced outside to be the first to the swings except for

Henry Hamster. He stayed behind in the classroom.

"Henry," said Miss Hummingbird, "why are you still inside? It's time for recess, go outside and play with your friends!"

"No thank you, I would rather just stay in here and play my new game." Henry took a small calculator sized gaming console out of his pocket and started playing a game where he had to stack as many blocks on top of each other without knocking the tower over.

All of his classmates were outside on the swings, playing tag, and tossing around a baseball. Everyone was laughing and having a blast, but Henry didn't feel like he was missing out, he loved playing video games.

The next day at recess the same thing happened. Everyone went outside to play, but Henry stayed in the classroom to play his video game.

"Henry, don't you miss playing with your friends?" Miss Hummingbird asked.

"I get to see them at lunch time and sometimes we go to each other's houses after school," Henry said without looking up from his game.

Miss Hummingbird was very concerned that Henry was not being active enough with all of the others in the class. So she decided to call home.

"Hi Mrs. Hamster, this is Miss Hummingbird. I'm Henry's school teacher."

"Hi Miss Hummingbird, how are you today?" Mrs. Hamster had a very pleasant voice.

"Well Mrs. Hamster, I'm a bit concerned about your son. He never goes outside at recess to play with his classmates. He just sits inside and plays video games all by himself. I think it might be affecting his friendships. Not to mention he isn't getting much physical activity, and we both know how important that is."

"Oh no!" Said Mrs. Hamster. "Henry's father and I have a limit on video games and we had no idea that he was sneaking games to school with him! We will make sure he doesn't have his games tomorrow. And yes, we do know how important it is that he goes outside, gets fresh air and exercise, and plays with all of this friends. Thank you very much for the phone call. I really appreciate it."

Mrs. Hamster kept her promise and the next day in school Henry Hamster had to go outside and play with his friends.

Francine Flamingo jumped onto the jungle gym and announced, "I am the queen of the playground and you are all my army! Go out and collect supplies to build my castle at once!"

Peter Penguin and Edgar Elephant bowed down and said, "Yes your highness!"

Henry Hamster just stared at them.

Peter Penguin waddled over to the bushes and started collecting leaves from the ground around them. "These shingles will build a strong roof for the castle!"

"Those are just leaves," said Henry Hamster.

Edgar Elephant was collecting sticks with his trunk. "These logs are huge and strong! They will make the walls of the castle and no enemy will ever break through!"

"Those aren't real logs," said Henry Hamster.

Francine Flamingo galloped over with a hockey stick between her legs and said, "I want you all to meet my royal steed!"

"That looks nothing like a horse!" Said Henry Hamster.

His three friends stared at him with confused looks.

"We're just using our imaginations, Henry, you should try it!" Francine Flamingo said. She handed him the hockey stick. "You can be the king of the playground and I'll let you ride my royal steed!"

Henry Hamster looked at the hockey stick, trying his hardest to make it look like a horse in his mind, but all he saw was a hockey stick. "Guys, I don't think I remember how to use my imagination!"

From all the hours Henry Hamster had spent playing video games, he became used to seeing things in front of his eyes. He hadn't used his imagination in weeks and now it was lost!

"Emergency!" Shouted Peter Penguin, "Dr. Elephant, do you think you can crack this case? It seems this young man has lost his imagination!"

"Hmmm..." Edgar Elephant used his trunk to tap on Henry's head. "It doesn't seem impossible, but we need to act quickly. Dr. Flamingo, can you assist me on the case?"

"Roger that!" Francine Flamingo began picking up rocks and sticks from the ground. "We've got all the tools we need right here!" She handed the rocks and sticks to Edgar.

Henry Hamster was staring at his friends like they were crazy, why were they acting like doctors?

As the game went on, Henry started to play along. He was surprised to find that he was starting to really feel like a patient. He started to call his friends Dr. Elephant and Dr. Flamingo. After several minutes of having the two of them poking at him and Peter fake crying off to the side, Henry realized it was all a game!

"Dr. Elephant. Dr. Flamingo. I am feeling so much better!"

Peter Penguin jumped up and said, "Are you healed, Henry?"

Henry smiled and picked up the hockey stick. "Go off and collect tools for the castle, it's not going to build itself! I will take this horse and go gather more supplies."

Everyone cheered and went back to playing the first game now that Henry Hamster had his imagination back. He realized that even though he really loved playing video games, he still needed to make time to play outside with his friends, and use his imagination. The more he used his imagination, the easier it got.

CHAPTER THREE

THE NEW KID

FRANCINE FLAMINGO, Edgar Elephant, Henry Hamster, and Peter Penguin were best friends. They were all in the same class and had been since preschool. Now they were in third grade. No one could break up their friend group and they didn't care to add anyone new.

Alexis Alligator was the new girl in class. She just moved to town from the Everglades.

"Class I want everyone to meet our new student Alexis Alligator!" Said Miss Hummingbird.

She called Alexis up to the front of the class to introduce herself.

"Hi," said Alexis Alligator, "I'm Alexis, but everyone calls me Alex. I'm from Florida. I like to swim." Alex Alligator talked very quietly, almost like she was whispering. She stared at the ground the whole time.

"Now, class," said Miss Hummingbird, "please be welcoming to Alex, it's not easy being at a new school and making new friends. Be sure to include her in your daily activities."

At lunch, later that day, the friends all sat together and Alex Alligator sat at the other end of the table all by herself.

"Where did she say she was from?" Asked Edgar Elephant.

"Florida," said Francine Flamingo.

"The Everglades to be exact," said Henry Hamster.

"Isn't that a swamp? Swamps are gross. She is probably dirty!" said Peter Penguin.

"Yeah," said Edgar, "my mom told me that there was an alligator family moving to town and she said I should be careful."

"My mom too," said Francine, "I heard that alligators from the Everglades are not nice at all. Apparently they like to attack people!"

Henry Hamster shuddered. "I hope she doesn't come for me first since I'm the smallest!" He said.

"Don't worry," said Peter, "we're your best friends and we won't let Alex Alligator anywhere near you."

Edgar and Francine nodded along.

Alex Alligator heard the entire conversation and it really hurt her feelings. She knew that they weren't trying to be mean, it's just that everyone had a judgment about what alligators were like. She knew people would be scared of her, but she hoped they would see that she was actually a very nice girl.

At recess, she decided to try to be friends with Francine Flamingo. Back in Florida, Alex had a friend named Frank and he was a Flamingo!

"Hi, I'm Alex."

Francine Flamingo jumped. She looked to her

left and to her right, but her friends were nowhere in sight because they were playing hide and seek.

"I had a friend back where I'm from and he was a Flamingo."

Francine Flamingo nodded and then she shouted, "ready or not, here I come!" And she ran off to find her friends.

Alex Alligator was left sitting all alone on a swing watching her classmates have fun. She felt left out but knew that she could always try again tomorrow.

When she got home that evening her dad asked how school was, but Alex Alligator ignored him and went straight to her bedroom and closed the door.

"Alex, what happened at school? Why are you

so sad?" Mr. Alligator followed Alex into her bedroom and sat down next to her.

"Everyone thinks I'm just another mean alligator and no one wants to be my friend."

"I'm sorry, honey, but we talked about this. Just keep being the great girl I know you are and soon they will see that not all alligators are mean."

The next day at school Alex Alligator tried to talk to Peter Penguin since they both probably liked to swim. They had desks next to each other in Miss Hummingbird's class. Alex leaned over and whispered, "Hi, I'm Alex. Do you like to swim too?"

Peter Penguin pretended not to hear her but he started thinking about what his mom had told him about alligators. They like to attack others and drag them to the bottom of the swamp to drown. Peter penguin thought that's what Alex Alligator was trying to do to him.

"How was school today?" Asked Mr. Alligator when Alex got home.

Alex Alligator started to cry. "They are all afraid of me because I'm different!"

Mr. Alligator was so heartbroken that his little girl was having a hard time so he decided that he would drive her to school the next day and talk to the teacher.

When Mr. Alligator and Alex Alligator pulled up to the school everyone was staring. Some people even pulled their children away. Mr. Alligator stomped right into the school to talk to Miss Hummingbird.

When he got to the classroom even Miss

Hummingbird seemed scared.

"I'm not going to hurt you," said Mr. Alligator. "Not all of us are mean like you think. I just want you to know that my daughter is having a hard time making friends because your class is fearful and judging her."

"Oh!" Exclaimed Miss Hummingbird, "I am so sorry, I will do my best to make sure Alex is included today."

"Thank you," said Mr. Alligator, and then he left Alex alone in the classroom to wait for the other students to arrive.

Henry Hamster was the first to get there and he was shaking because he was so scared to be alone in the room with Alex Alligator. Miss Hummingbird had gone down the hall to the bathroom.

"Hi!" Said Alex.

Henry squeaked out a timid hello. He didn't want to make her angry.

"You're Henry, right?"

Henry nodded.

"I noticed that you were wearing a speed race t-shirt, do you play that video game?"

Henry nodded.

"I love that game, it's probably my favorite. What is your favorite race track?"

Henry squeaked, "I like the rings of Saturn."

"Yeah!" Said Alex, "that is such a fun one! Maybe you can come over after school one day and we can play!"

Henry felt his little hamster tummy get all tied up in a knot because he was so scared. "I don't think my parents would let me go to your house."

"Are you afraid of me?" Asked Alex Alligator.

Henry nodded.

"You shouldn't be scared. I'm not mean, I'm actually very nice. I moved here because my dad didn't want me to become mean like the other kids in my class, he wanted me to see that there are other ways to live."

"So you don't want to eat me?" Asked Henry.

"I'm actually a vegetarian!"

"Me too!" Said Henry.

Then they started talking about their favorite vegetables and Henry felt a lot better. He decided that he would go over to Alex's house after school. He felt bad that he judged her without getting to know her and promised to always give new friends a chance because that's what he would want if he were a new kid in town. Just because Alex was an Alligator didn't mean that she was like the bad Alligator's he had heard about.

When the others came in the classroom, Henry explained to them that Alex was nice after all and he told them that they didn't need to be afraid of her.

"We need to remember the Golden Rule. To treat others, the way we would like to be treated. We need to start treating Alex the way we would like to be treated." He reminded them. So they all sat together at lunch and asked Alex some fun questions to get to know her better. And at recess, they all laughed and played together. They decided as a group that the more friends the merrier.

Chapter Four

SCRUB-A-DUB-DUB

FRANCINE FLAMINGO WAS A tomboy. Until Alex Alligator moved to town, all of Francine's friends were boys and she liked it that way. She preferred to run around and play sports while the other girls in the class liked to do other activities.

During a big rainstorm, all of the friends

decided to go stomp in puddles. By the time Francine Flamingo got back home, her pink feathers had disappeared under a coat of brown clay.

"Honey, you need to go take a bath!" Said her parents.

Francine knew that she couldn't go to sleep until the mud was off her, but she was so sleepy from all the fun she had had. She felt too tired to take a bath, so instead, she just used a damp wash towel to wipe most of the dirt off. Once she was pink again, she went to bed.

They next morning, when she finished her cereal, her mom told her to go brush her teeth before heading to school. Francine didn't want to waste time brushing her teeth. She liked to play outside on the playground before going into class. If she brushed her teeth, she wouldn't have as much time to do that. Besides, she could just brush them when she got home.

During recess, all of her friends were running around playing tag. The sun was beating down on them and it was making Francine Flamingo kind of sweaty. It felt good to be back inside the cool classroom afterward.

When she got home that night her mom said, "Francine Flamingo, you stink!"

Francine shrugged. She didn't care, because she had had so much fun!

"Go take a bath," her mother demanded.

Francine filled up the tub and sat in the water until she got bored. She didn't use soap or shampoo because that would take too much time. She wanted to have enough time to watch TV before bed. The water washed off most of the stink. After, she turned on the TV and watched it until she fell asleep. And because she fell asleep, she forgot to go back and brush her teeth!

"Time for school Francine!" Her mother called upstairs to wake her up the next morning and Francine came to the kitchen to have breakfast.

"Make sure you brush your teeth before you go. You need to brush two times a day!"

Francine went to the bathroom and ran the sink to make her mother think she was brushing and then ran off to school.

"What's that smell?" Alex Alligator was sniffing the air.

Francine Flamingo knew it was probably her bad breath, so she didn't answer.

"Smells like someone passed gas!" Said Edgar Elephant.

"Ew!"

During recess, they all played tag again. Now everyone had bad breath because they ate lunch. After everyone was sweaty from running around, they headed back into class.

"Francine Flamingo, you stink!" Gasped Miss Flamingo when Francine walked in the front door after school. "Go take a bath before dinner!"

Again, Francine filled up the tub and just soaked in the water. She didn't feel like using shampoo or soap. Water would wash off the stink. After sitting in the bath for five minutes she went down for dinner.

"Francine Flamingo, you still stink! Did you

really take a bath?"

"Yes."

"Well, you need to go right back up there and take another one."

This time, Francine used soap to scrub her underarms, but nothing else. It covered up most of the stink, but by the time she got to school the next day, she was already sweaty from the hot sunshine.

Again, her friends started to sniff the air and question what the awful smell was.

At recess, everyone decided not to play tag. They wanted to play hide and seek instead. Edgar Elephant was the first seeker and when he closed his eyes to count, everyone ran off to hide. Edgar found everyone except Francine but he didn't want to try to find her.

"Did you guys notice that Francine is the one who smells bad?" He asked.

Everyone nodded.

"I'm just going to let her stay hidden until recess is over so that we don't have to smell her. She will just think she had the best hiding spot."

Everyone agreed.

When the bell rang to signal that recess was over, Francine Flamingo jumped out from under the slide. "You couldn't find me! Hah!" She mocked Edgar Elephant for not being able to find her and he just held his breath.

In class, her classmates all inched their desks away from her and she didn't know why.

Then Miss Hummingbird told the class to pair up. Henry Hamster and Edgar Elephant were partners. Peter Penguin and Alex Alligator were partners. Francine Flamingo didn't know why none of her friends wanted to be her partner.

"We can just be a group of three!" She said.

"Actually, Francine Flamingo, can I speak with you?" Miss Hummingbird called her out into the hallway.

"I noticed that you may have forgotten to bathe yourself this morning and a lot of your classmates have complained. Your mom is on her way to pick you up."

Francine Flamingo was so embarrassed. She didn't notice that she smelled that bad because she was used to it. Turns out, brushing your teeth and taking baths was important and not just something her mom forced her to do. She decided that it was just as easy to wash up as it was to just sit still in the bath water. And it didn't take that much longer to do. She promised Miss Hummingbird that it would never happen again and when she got home she took a long bath and scrubbed every inch of her feathers twice! Surprisingly, she felt and smelled better because of it.

Chapter Five

IT FEELS GOOD TO GIVE

MISS HUMMINGBIRD DECIDED to plan a field trip for her class. Over the past few weeks, she noticed that her class was becoming restless.

Peter Penguin never paid attention and instead of taking notes he drew cartoons in his notebook.

Francine Flamingo kept falling asleep in class.

Edgar Elephant and Alex Alligator were passing notes back and forth.

Henry Hamster was hiding his video games in his desk and playing them during Miss Hummingbirds lessons.

"Class, who knows the answer to this question: who was the first president?"

No one raised their hands, it was like they didn't even hear her.

When the lunch bell rang everyone got up and went to the cafeteria. Miss Hummingbird wondered if she stopped teaching if anyone would even notice. So while the class was out at lunch and recess, Miss Hummingbird took all the books off the shelves and hid them under her desk. She took all the toys from the indoor play time station and hid them in the storage closet. When the class got back from recess they took their seats and got back to doodling, passing notes, napping, and playing video games.

Miss Hummingbird sat at her desk at the front of the room and started to read the newspaper.

After a few minutes, Edgar Elephant spoke up and said, "Miss Hummingbird, are you going to teach us something?"

Miss Hummingbird didn't respond she just said, "Field trip tomorrow. You all can play."

The students were confused, but they weren't going to turn down play time. They all went over to the play time station, but the toys were all gone.

"Miss Hummingbird, where are all the toys?"

"We don't have toys here anymore."

The kids were disappointed and went over to the bookshelves, if there were no toys, they might as well read.

"Miss Hummingbird, where are all the books?"

"No books in this school."

The class was disappointed and they all went back to their desks and sat around feeling bored while waiting for the bell to ring so they could all go home.

The next day in school everyone boarded a bus for the field trip, but they had no idea where Miss Hummingbird was taking them!

The bus pulled up to a children's hospital and all of the students felt confused.

"Miss Hummingbird," said Francine Flamingo, "why are we at the hospital? Is someone we know sick?"

"Nope."

When they walked into the hospital there were a lot of kids their ages hanging out in the recreation room. Some of them had casts on and some of them were on crutches.

Miss Hummingbird brought out a box and said to her class, "The children in the hospital don't get to go to school because they need to heal."

One of the patients walked by and overheard Miss Hummingbird talking. "It's true," he said. "I miss going to school. It's hard doing my school work without the help of my teacher. I can't wait to go back."

The students were shocked, they thought all kids got to go to school every day.

"And because they need to do their schoolwork in the hospital," Miss Hummingbird added, "they need books and toys, but unfortunately, the hospital sometimes cannot afford to buy them."

"Wow," said Henry Hamster.

"Remember how boring yesterday was when we had no toys and books?" Asked Edgar Elephant.

Miss Hummingbird opened the box and said, "I thought it might be nice to donate some of the books and toys from our classroom to the children here. Sometimes we forget how fortunate we are, and we can take the things we have for granted."

Everyone was so excited to give to the kids in

the hospital. They didn't realize that there were less fortunate people out there and felt bad that they took all of the good things in their lives for granted. As they saw the excitement on all of the patient's faces, they decided that they wanted to go back to school and find more things to give and donate. Giving felt good! "I think I am going to go home and gather even more things to donate!" said Francine Flamingo. "And I can't wait to go back to school and hear what Miss Hummingbird is going to teach us next." Said Peter Penguin.

CHAPTER SIX

LET'S STAY UP ALL NIGHT

DURING THE WEEKEND, everyone likes to have slumber parties. Francine Flamingo and Alex Alligator had one at Francine's house and all the boys were over at Henry Hamster's house.

The big challenge was to stay up all night long. When everyone was back at school on Monday they would exchange stories about what time they finally went to sleep and whoever stayed up the longest had bragging rights for the week.

Francine Flamingo and Alex Alligator planned to watch movies all night and eat snacks. There were bottles of soda and bags of chips to last them the whole night. They put in a movie and snuggled up with blankets and poured themselves a glass of soda.

"The soda will help us stay awake," said Alex.

"We will definitely beat the boys!" Said Francine.

Over at the other slumber party, all of the boys were huddled around Henry Hamster's video game console drinking energy drinks.

"This game is so fun and exciting it will totally keep us up all night!" Said Henry.

Edgar Elephant and Peter Penguin agreed.

The sun went down and the clock ticked on and on until it was well pass midnight. Everyone started getting very sleepy, but they just drank more soda and energy drinks to help keep them awake.

After a few more hours, Peter Penguin started to nod off.

"Stay strong Peter! You can stay awake!" Said Henry Hamster, but Peter Penguin started snoring. He was the first to fall asleep.

Over at the girls' slumber party, both girls were yawning.

"Maybe we should just go to sleep," said Alex Alligator.

"Do you think the boys are still awake?" Asked Francine Flamingo.

"I'm so tired, I don't think I care."

It was almost two in the morning when they finally gave in. Both girls crawled into their sleeping bags and slept until the morning.

After Peter Penguin fell asleep, Edgar Elephant and Henry Hamster tried their hardest to stay awake. They each drank another energy drink and started playing another video game.

"I'm feeling very tired, and my stomach kind of hurts." said Edgar Elephant.

"Drink another energy drink, we are going to stay awake until the sun comes up!" Said Henry Hamster.

They stayed awake and played video games and drank energy drinks until the sun rose. In the morning, everyone went back to their own houses.

Peter Penguin went out and raked his neighbors leaves. He was awake because he was the first one to fall asleep, therefore, he had had enough sleep.

Alex Alligator did her homework, but she felt very tired, therefore, she had a hard time concentrating and it made her get some of her answers wrong.

Francine Flamingo had a headache, so she took a nap, but then she didn't even get a chance to do her homework.

Edgar Elephant slept all day and then missed school on Monday.

Henry Hamster figured, since he was up all night, he might as well keep going until bedtime. He played video games for the entire day.

On Monday, back in school, Peter Penguin was able to answer all the questions that Miss Hummingbird asked.

Alex Alligator got her first bad grade on a homework assignment.

Francine Flamingo got in trouble for not doing her homework assignment.

Edgar Elephant stayed home because he missed the bus.

Henry Hamster was in class but he had a runny nose and could barely pay attention because he kept falling asleep!

He went to the school nurse to tell him that he didn't feel very well.

"I think I'm coming down with a cold," said Henry Hamster.

Mr. Rabbit took Henry's temperature and said, "I think you have a bit of a fever Henry Hamster, I'm going to call your mom to have her come pick you up and take you home."

When Henry Hamster got home he crawled into his bed and slept the rest of the day and all through the night.

He woke up feeling a lot better and went back to school.

"What happened, Henry?" Alex Alligator asked.

"I got sick because I didn't get enough sleep at the slumber party. And the energy drinks aren't very healthy either."

"I failed my homework because I didn't get enough sleep at the slumber party. It was like my brain was in a big fog," said Francine Flamingo.

"Well, I'm sure glad that I listened to my body and went to sleep when I did!" Peter Penguin said. "I feel great!"

The next weekend when everyone was having slumber parties, they didn't even try to stay up all night long. When they felt tired, they turned out the lights and went to sleep. No one wanted to take the chance of getting sick or doing badly in school. They learned their lesson that getting enough sleep is very important.

AFTERWORD

Thanks again for picking up this book! You are participating in making our world a better place.

For more of our Karma for Kids books please visit us at:

www.karmaforkidsbooks.wordpress.com
or
www.findyourwaypublishing.com

Find Norma MacDonald and her books online at Amazon.com.

Other books that we recommend to help children learn important life lessons:

Billy Brown Bear and Friends; Short Stories, Fuzzy Animals, and Life Lessons by Norma MacDonald

Humble Heron and Friends; Short Stories, Fuzzy Animals, and Life Lessons by Norma MacDonald

Guaranteed Success for Kindergarten; 50 Easy Things You Can Do Today! by Marrae Kimball

Guaranteed Success for Grade School; 50 Easy Things You Can Do Today! by Marrae Kimball

The Secret Combination to Middle School: Real Advice from Real Kids, Ideas for Success, and Much More! by Marrae Kimball

NORMA MACDONALD

We love reviews and we would love to know how you liked the stories. Please feel free to contact us!

If you have ideas for stories, please feel free to share and send them to:

Melissa Eshleman
Find Your Way Publishing, Inc.
PO Box 667
Norway, ME 04268
Melissa@findyourwaypublishing.com

www.findyourwaypublishing.com

Thank you!

NORMA MACDONALD

PETER PENGUIN AND FRIENDS

Printed in Great Britain
by Amazon